SPLASH AND DASH

by Mickie Matheis

illustrated by Kellee Riley

PENGUIN YOUNG READERS LICENSES
An Imprint of Penguin Random House

PENGUIN YOUNG READERS LICENSES
An Imprint of Penguin Random House LLC

© 2018. All rights reserved. HATCHIMALS™ is
a trademark of Spin Master Ltd., used under license. Published by
Penguin Young Readers Licenses, an imprint of Penguin Random House LLC,
345 Hudson Street, New York, New York 10014. Manufactured in China.

ISBN 9781524787165   10 9 8 7 6 5 4 3 2 1

Olivia the Octapitta was juggling pebbles
in the sparkling sands of Breezy Beach.
As the waves crashed ashore behind her,
a crowd of Hatchimals chanted
her name: "Olivia! Olivia! Olivia!"

It was *hatchtastic* watching eight shiny
pebbles fly smoothly through the air!

For her big finish, Olivia tossed the eight pebbles up high and prepared to catch
them all on the tip of one tentacle. But just then, two energetic Crablers playing
tag scampered by and accidentally kicked sand in Olivia's face. One by one,
the pebbles fell, bonking her on her head.

"Ouch!" said the Octapitta, rubbing the sore spot.

"Olivia! OLIVIA!" a voice said loudly. Confused, Olivia opened her eyes. Why was the crowd still calling her name?

She saw her best friend, Pete the Penguala, peering at her as she lay in her cozy coral nest. "Can you practice with me now?" he asked. "Beach Blast is tomorrow."

4

I was just dreaming, Olivia realized. It was time to get up and help her friend prepare for Beach Blast, which was a part of the Hatchy Games, an annual competition in Hatchtopia. Everyone expected Pete to win many golden seashell medals for the different aquatic events taking place at Breezy Beach. The daredevil Penguala loved extreme sports—especially surfing giant ocean waves! He also hoped to take home the grand prize awarded at the conclusion of Beach Blast: the Super Starfish Trophy.

Olivia felt too shy to enter the competition. But she knew it was important to Pete, so she had promised she would help him train.

"Let's start with the Seashell Toss," suggested Olivia. She searched the sand until she found a seashell that was just the right size. "Ready?" she asked, and tossed it to Pete. He caught it easily. Again and again, Olivia threw the seashell until Pete was catching everything that came his way.

"*EGGcellent!*" Olivia exclaimed. "You're ready for the Seashell Toss!"

Next, Olivia and Pete headed to the ocean to prepare for the Saltwater Swim.

As she watched Pete practice, Olivia called out helpful hints. Soon, the Penguala was darting through the water as fast as any fish.

Olivia dived into the ocean to race her friend. By the third try, Pete beat the swift Octapitta by a wing tip. "Great job!" Olivia told him.

"Thank you! I feel much better about the Saltwater Swim now," Pete said. Olivia was a very good coach!

As she glided back toward shore, Olivia grabbed a bunch of seaweed. She tied it together like a rope and handed one end to Pete. It was time to practice the Seaweed Tug-of-War.

The two friends stood in the sand. "Three . . . two . . . one!" Olivia counted, then pulled. Pete felt himself being dragged forward. He grunted and tugged back. The Octapitta was super strong!

Olivia gave the seaweed a hard yank, and the Penguala toppled over. Pete laughed as he wiped off his beak and stood up. They tried again, and this time, Pete dug his webbed feet deep into the sand. When Olivia pulled, he didn't budge. Several practice rounds later, Pete felt prepared for the Seaweed Tug-of-War.

The fourth event was the Sandsational Sandcastle Contest. Whichever Hatchimal built the most creative sandcastle before time ran out would win.

"Courtney the Crabler will be the hardest to beat," warned Olivia. "She builds the biggest, fanciest sandcastles."

The two friends stayed in the sand for a long time designing different sandcastles. By late afternoon, Olivia declared the Penguala ready to compete.

The next morning, the sun shone brightly over Breezy Beach, and a light wind blew from the ocean. It was a perfect day!

Preparation for the games had begun early. A Sealark named Shelly was in charge and had spent the morning with her crew moving equipment to the proper places.

Skylar, a Skunkle and an award-winning photographer, was unpacking a large camera bag. Her job was to capture all the action.

"Good morning, everyone!" said Daya the Dragonflip. This chatty, cheerful Hatchimal had come to provide commentary on the events. Normally, she made the morning announcements at the Daisy Schoolhouse, so she was looking forward to this special assignment.

Contestants were warming up across Breezy Beach. Some swam in the ocean. Others ran along the shore. There was even a group doing exercises led by Hannah, a Hummingbear who taught gym class at the Daisy Schoolhouse.

Olivia had arrived early. She looked around for her Penguala pal, but he was nowhere to be seen.

Suddenly, a shout came from the water. Pete was surfing toward shore on a giant wave—while doing a handstand!

"What are you doing?" Olivia called out nervously. She didn't think it was a good time for stunt-surfing.

"Hatching some waves!" he yelled back. Pete didn't realize that he was headed straight for a bunch of hatchlings taking synchronized swimming lessons.

When he finally noticed, he had to turn his surfboard hard to avoid crashing into them. As he tumbled into the shallow water, he jammed his wing on his board.

"Oh no!" Olivia cried, running over to her friend. She gently took his wing to examine it. "Are you okay?"

"It really hurts," the Penguala replied as he tried bending it. "I don't think I can compete."

"But you've worked so hard," Olivia protested.

"You're going to have to win some medals for me," Pete said. "Take my place, Olivia. You helped me train. You can do it!"

Olivia didn't feel particularly confident, but she agreed to try for her friend.

"I'll be right here, rooting you on," Pete promised.

The first event was the Saltwater Swim. All the best swimmers from Hatchtopia were there, including a Swhale, a Platypiper, and a Dolfinch.

Daya called out the rules. "You will start at the shoreline and swim out to that sandbar," she said, pointing about two miles away. "Then race back. The first one to cross the finish line wins."

When the whistle blew, Olivia launched herself into the water, rocketing through it at tremendous speed. Soon she felt the grainy sandbar. She did a perfect underwater flip and propelled herself back toward shore.

Before she knew it, she had reached the beach, and she could hear the chant of "Olivia! Olivia! Olivia!"—just like in her dream! Pete and a crowd of Hatchimals were cheering for her. When she turned around, she saw how far away all the other swimmers were. Olivia had not just won the race—she had won it by a mile! The first golden seashell medal was hers.

The next event was the Seashell Toss. Hatchimals lined up in two rows facing one another. Olivia was across from a Tigrette named Tommy. He was the best baskEGGball player in all of Hatchtopia.

"You can do it, Olivia—just like we practiced!" Pete yelled encouragingly.

The whistle blew, signaling the start of the event.

Contestants had to toss the seashell directly to their opponents. Each time the seashell was caught, they took a step back. As the distance between players grew, it became increasingly more difficult to catch the tosses.

Of course, Tommy turned out to be very skilled at the Seashell Toss, but Olivia discovered that she was also quite good. Her long, nimble tentacles were perfect for catching Tommy's tosses. Maybe she could win this event, too!

After a while, only Olivia and Tommy were left playing. The pair had just taken another step backward when Tommy finally missed a toss. The crowd gasped. They thought Tommy would win for sure. "Now, remember . . . you must catch this one in order to win," Daya reminded Olivia.

"You've got this, Olivia!" Pete yelled.

Tommy's next throw came low and fast at Olivia. She could tell the seashell was going to fall a bit short from where she stood, so she lunged forward. She managed to catch it but couldn't hang on to it. She felt the shell slip from her tentacle, but before it hit the sand, she scooped it up with another tentacle. Olivia held the seashell high for all to see. She had won!

"Good game, Olivia!" Tommy said, walking over to shake one of her tentacles. "You've got awesome reflexes. You should come play baskEGGball sometime."

"Thanks, Tommy, maybe I will," Olivia said happily.

Pete congratulated his best friend on another victory. "You're doing so well!" he said, hugging her.

"And I'm having fun!" she admitted as she received another golden seashell medal.

The Hatchimals were paired up once again for the Seaweed Tug-of-War. This time, they stood on opposite sides of a line of seashells in the sand.

Olivia was matched up with a Kittycan named Katie. "Good luck!" the Kittycan said cheerily. Olivia had never met Katie before, but she had heard of her. The Meadow Hatchimal was known for her love of the Hatchy Games. When she put her mind to winning, she usually did!

The whistle blew. Almost immediately, Katie dragged the Octapitta within a few inches of the seashells.

Olivia regained her footing and held tightly to the seaweed rope. Neither the Octapitta nor the Kittycan managed to move the other any farther.

Finally, Olivia's tentacles needed a rest, so she began to reposition herself. That's when Katie made her move, darting into the air while giving a hard pull. Olivia wasn't expecting this and stumbled forward, crossing the line of seashells. The Kittycan had won!

"Wow, Olivia, you are a tough tug-of-war opponent!" Katie said, congratulating her with an enthusiastic hatch five. "You put up such a good fight."

"Thanks, Katie," Olivia replied. She felt a little disappointed that she had lost the match.

Pete tried to cheer her up. "Don't be sad. You did a great job! You can still win the last event."

But Olivia was worried about the Sandsational Sandcastle Contest. While she was very fast at building sandcastles because of her eight tentacles, she wondered what she could do to make her castle stand out—especially against Courtney the Crabler and her fancy creations.

All she could do was try her best, she reminded herself. And she knew she had Pete cheering her on.

For the sandcastle contest, each Hatchimal was given a bucket, a shovel, several sticks, a piece of colored cloth, and some pebbles and shells.

The whistle blew, and Olivia got to work. One tentacle held the bucket while two tentacles scooped and shoveled sand into it. The other five tentacles worked quickly to pour and shape the castle. Walls flew up, followed by towers, a moat, and a drawbridge.

Olivia's castle construction was going well, and there was still plenty of time left. She might just have a chance at winning after all!

She was about to begin building a spiral staircase when one of her tentacles bumped something in the sand. "Oh! It's an egg!" she cried, patting it gently. *Tap-tap. Tap-tap-tap.* The heart on the egg was purple. That meant it needed help hatching.

Olivia hesitated. If she stopped to help the egg hatch, she might not finish her sandcastle. But she quickly decided that being a good friend to another Hatchimal was far more important. So the Octapitta grabbed the colored cloth, wrapped the egg in it, and held it tightly against her. "Come out, come out, whoever you are," the Octapitta cooed as she rocked the egg.

Pete hurried over to help. His friendly voice combined with Olivia's cuddling did the trick. After a few minutes of both of them encouraging and rubbing the egg, the heart turned pink.

Seconds later, the egg began to crack, and a head popped out of the top. "It's an Elefly!" Olivia said. "Hatchy Birthday—I'm going to name you Ella."

A Dolfinch named Duncan came over carrying a seashell crown. "Welcome!" he said, gently placing the crown on the head of the newest Hatchimal. Ella waddled over to the sandcastle and sat down on a shell, smiling at the crowd that had gathered.

Olivia picked up a stick and attached a sand dollar to it. Then the Octapitta gently tied some seaweed around the little Elefly. "There you are, Your Majesty," she laughed.

Suddenly, a buzzer sounded. "Time's up!" Daya announced.

Olivia looked over at Courtney the Crabler's sandcastle. She had sculpted a huge castle with majestic mountains and had used pebbles to outline windows, doors, and walking paths. Colorful flags flew from all the spires. It was spectacular!

Olivia's heart sank. "I'm sorry, Pete," she said. "My castle will never beat that."

"That's okay, Olivia," Pete assured her. "Ella needed your help to hatch. That was more important. You did the right thing."

Daya was ready to announce the winner.
"We have a tie!" she proclaimed.
"The judges are awarding medals to
Courtney and Olivia for the best sandcastles."
"Hooray!" yelled Pete, throwing his good
wing in the air.
Olivia couldn't believe her ears.
"But . . . how?" she asked, confused.

"The judges thought it was very clever that your castle had its very own queen!" Daya explained as she hung a golden seashell medal around Olivia's neck. "That made your castle special. Congratulations!"

"Courtney, your castle is incredible," Olivia told the Yellow Crabler.

"But yours is incredibly creative," Courtney said. "You definitely deserve that medal!"

And that wasn't all. The judges also awarded the Super Starfish Trophy to Olivia for being the MVP of Beach Blast. "That stands for Most Valuable Pal—because being a good friend and helping Ella to hatch was more important than finishing your sandcastle," Daya explained.

Olivia draped one of her medals around Ella and snuggled her tightly. Then she removed another medal and placed it around Pete's neck.

Skylar the Skunkle scooted over to snap a photograph of the happy trio.

"I'm so proud of you, Olivia," Pete said.

"Thanks, Pete!" Olivia replied. "I'm so glad I competed today. I never thought I would be brave enough!"

Pete smiled. "But you were! You have a kind heart, too. And that's why you'll always be a winner!"